The Water Of Life

The Water Of Life

A TALE FROM THE BROTHERS GRIMM

· RETOLD BY ·

Barbara Rogasky

· ILLUSTRATED BY ·

Trina Schart Hyman

Holiday House

NEW YORK   1986 A.D.

Library of Congress Cataloging in Publication Data

Rogasky, Barbara.
The water of life.

Adaptation of Das Wasser des Lebens by Jacob and Wilhelm Grimm.
SUMMARY: A prince searching for the Water of Life to
cure his dying father finds an enchanted castle, a lovely
princess, and treachery from his older brothers.
[1. Fairy tales. 2. Folklore—Germany] I. Hyman,
Trina Schart, ill. II. Grimm, Jacob, 1785–1863. Wasser
des Lebens. III. Title.
PZ8.R618Wat 1986   398.2'6'0943 [E]   84-19226
ISBN 0-8234-0552-4

For my sister MURIEL

B.R.

For BARBARA

T.S.H.

Once upon a time there was a king who became so sick that everyone believed he would die. His three sons were very sad. One day they went to the castle gardens, where they wept in sorrow.

A little old man came over to them and asked, "Why are you crying?"

They explained that their father was dying of a terrible sickness, and that there was no cure.

"I know a cure," said the little old man. "It's the Water of Life. If he drinks it, the king will be well again. But it is very hard to find."

The oldest son said, "I'll find it." He went to his father to ask permission.

The king shook his head weakly. "No," he said. "The danger is too great. I would rather die."

The son begged and pleaded, telling his father how much he loved him. But secretly he thought, "If I find this Water of Life and my father is cured, he will leave his kingdom to me when he dies."

The king believed his son's love was pure, and finally he gave his permission.

The prince set off on his journey. In a little while, he came upon a dwarf who stood in the middle of the road. "Where are you going so fast?" the dwarf asked.

The prince, who had to stop his horse, was greatly annoyed. "Stupid runt," he said. "That's no business of yours." And he rode proudly away, his nose in the air.

The little man was very angry, and he cursed the king's oldest son.

Soon the prince came to a steep-sided ravine between two mountains. As he rode along, the ravine became narrower and narrower, until it was barely wide enough for the prince and his horse to pass through. Finally it became so narrow that they got stuck. No matter how much he pushed or poked or prodded or yelled, the prince and his horse could move neither forward nor backward. So there they stayed, wedged between the walls of the ravine.

The king waited a long time for his oldest son to return, but he did not come back. And the king grew sicker and sicker.

One day his second son came to him and asked permission to look for the Water of Life.

Weaker than ever, the king shook his head. "No," he said. "The danger is too great. I would rather die."

"Please, Father," his second son said. "Let me go out of love for you." But to himself he was saying, as his brother had said, "If I find this Water of Life and my father is cured, the kingdom will be mine when he dies."

The king believed his second son's love was pure, and at last he gave his permission.

The prince set off. Before long, he too came upon the dwarf standing in the middle of the road. "Where are you going so fast?" the dwarf asked.

The prince had stopped his horse. "Idiot midget," he said. "That's none of your business." And he almost ran over the dwarf in his proud haste to get away.

The tiny man, angry again, cursed the king's second son.

The prince came to a steep-sided ravine, and the same thing happened. The farther he rode, the narrower it became, until finally he was stuck fast and could move neither forward nor backward. This is what happens to those who have too much pride.

When the second son did not return, the youngest went to his father and asked his leave to seek the Water of Life. So weak he could barely speak, the king gave his permission.

On his journey the prince came upon the dwarf, who asked him where he was hurrying so fast. He stopped the horse and explained. "I am searching for the Water of Life, because my father is so sick he is dying."

"Do you know how to find it?" the dwarf asked.

"No," said the prince.

"Since you have not been too proud to answer me, the way your brothers were," the dwarf said, "I'll tell you where the Water of Life is and help you get it. There is a fountain in the courtyard of an enchanted castle, and the Water of Life flows from that. But you will never get in unless you do exactly as I say."

The prince listened carefully.

The dwarf said, "Here is an iron rod and two loaves of bread. Knock on the castle gate three times with the rod, and it will open. In the courtyard there are two lions with huge gaping jaws. Throw a loaf of bread to each one and they will calm down and let you pass. Then hurry and take the Water of Life. You must leave with it before the clock strikes twelve or the gate will close and lock you inside."

The prince thanked him, took the iron rod and two loaves of bread, and went on his way.

Everything happened as the dwarf had said. The prince knocked three times with the iron rod and the castle gate flew open. In the courtyard lay two lions with their huge mouths open and their sharp teeth glistening. He threw each a loaf of bread and they quieted down.

The prince walked into the castle. He came to a big hall, where many enchanted princes sat around a long table. They did not move, nor did they speak. The king's youngest son took the rings from each one's fingers, and picked up a sword and a loaf of bread that lay near them on the floor.

In the next room, he found the most beautiful princess he had ever seen. He fell in love with her then and there.

The princess was so happy to see him that she kissed him joyously. "You have set me free," she said. "If you come back to me in a year we will marry and my kingdom will be yours."

Then she told him how to find the hidden courtyard where the Water of Life flowed. "But hurry. You must draw the water before the clock strikes twelve."

The prince promised to return in a year's time, and went on.

Along his way, he came into a room that held a freshly made bed. It looked so inviting, and he was so tired, that he lay down and fell asleep.

He awoke with a start as the clock was striking a quarter to twelve. He jumped from the bed in fright and ran into the courtyard of the castle.

There stood the fountain, and from it flowed the Water of Life. He quickly filled a cup with the precious liquid and, just as the clock was striking twelve, left through the castle gate. On the last stroke, the gate closed with such force that it took off a piece of his heel.

All the same he was happy to have the Water of Life, and he started homeward to his father.

After a while he met the dwarf again, and he stopped to thank him. When the dwarf saw the sword and the loaf of bread, he said, "The sword and loaf of bread will be great treasures to you. The sword can defeat entire armies, and the loaf of bread will never grow smaller no matter how much is taken from it."

The prince did not want to go home to his father without his brothers. "Good dwarf," he said, "do you know where my brothers are? They set out before me to find the Water of Life, but they have never returned."

The dwarf said, "They are stuck fast, wedged between two mountains. I cursed them, because they were so proud."

The prince begged the dwarf to release them, and at last the dwarf set them free. But he warned the prince, "Beware of your brothers. They have evil hearts."

Nonetheless the prince was glad to see his brothers again. They listened closely as he told them about finding the Water of Life and filling a cup with the liquid to take to their dying father. They bent their heads to hear when he described the beautiful princess and told them of her promise to marry him and make him prince of a great kingdom if he returned in a year's time.

Then the three of them rode away together on the long trip home.

They came to a land where war and famine raged. Destruction and starvation so afflicted the place that its king believed all was lost. The youngest son went to him and gave him the loaf of bread. With it the king fed his entire kingdom, and yet the loaf of bread remained whole. The prince then gave him the sword, and with that the king destroyed the invading armies and peace reigned over the land.

The prince took back the loaf and the sword, and the three brothers rode on. Twice more on their journey they came to lands that war and famine had brought nearly to ruin. Each time the prince lent the king the loaf of bread and the sword, and each time the people were fed and the kingdom was saved. But the loaf remained whole, and the sword did not stop shining.

In this way, the youngest prince saved three kingdoms and earned the eternal gratitude of three kings.

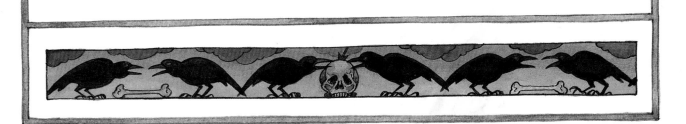

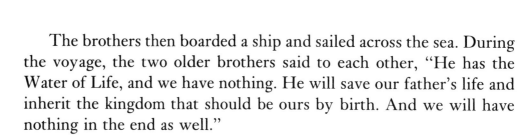

The brothers then boarded a ship and sailed across the sea. During the voyage, the two older brothers said to each other, "He has the Water of Life, and we have nothing. He will save our father's life and inherit the kingdom that should be ours by birth. And we will have nothing in the end as well."

They burned with anger and yearned for revenge. Together they plotted to destroy their youngest brother. While he slept, they emptied the Water of Life from his cup and poured it into one of their own. Then they filled his cup with bitter sea water.

As soon as they arrived home, the youngest son went to his father. He gave him the cup that he believed held the Water of Life, expecting him to drink from it and become well again. But instead, the king took a sip, spat the bitterness out of his mouth, and grew sicker than before.

As he lay in misery, the two older sons came in to him and accused their younger brother of trying to poison him.

"We have the Water of Life," they said, and gave their cup to the king. The moment he took one swallow, his sickness began to leave him. Before long he was as healthy and strong as he had been in the days of his youth.

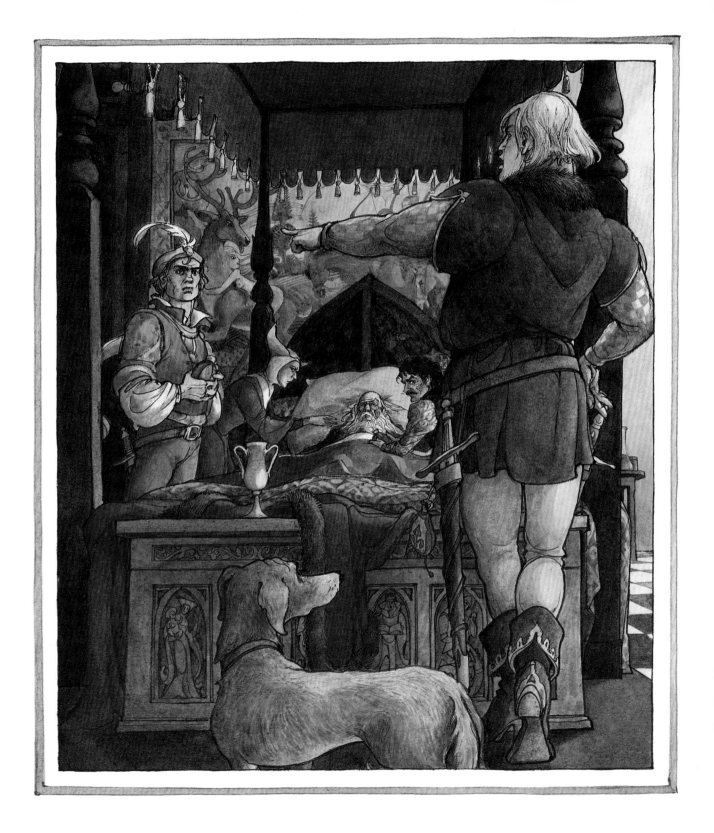

When the two older brothers saw the youngest son, they laughed at him. "You found the Water of Life, but we took it away from you. You did all the work, but we will get all the reward. You should have kept your eyes open—we took it from you while you were asleep.

"Not only that," they said to him, "in a year one of us will go to the beautiful princess and claim her. One of us will be prince of her kingdom, not you.

"Furthermore," they said, "do not go to the king our father and tell him what we have done. He thinks you have betrayed him and he will not believe you.

"Besides that," they said, "if you say one word, we will kill you. If you want to live, you must keep silent."

The king, now restored to strength, was furious at his youngest son, who he thought had tried to murder him. So the king called his council together, and they sentenced the youngest prince to be shot in secret.

The prince suspected nothing. One day he went hunting, and the king's huntsman was ordered to go with him. When they were deep in the forest, the prince saw that the huntsman looked very sad.

"Good huntsman," he said, "what is the matter?"

"I must not tell you," the huntsman answered, "and yet I should."

"Say whatever it is. I swear I will forgive you," the prince said.

"Alas, my prince! I must kill you. The king your father has commanded it."

Filled with horror, the prince said, "Huntsman, do not kill me! Give me my life."

"Dear prince, I must kill you," the huntsman said sadly, and he raised his gun.

"Wait!" the prince said. "Stop! Give me your huntsman's clothes and take my royal garments in exchange, and I will escape into the forest."

"With gladness," the huntsman said. "I would never have been able to shoot you."

And so the huntsman went home by back roads where no one would see him in the prince's clothes, and the prince wandered deeper into the forest disguised in the simple clothes of the huntsman.

Some time after this, three wagons filled with gold and jewels came to the king for his youngest son. They were sent in gratitude from the three kings whose kingdoms the prince had saved with his sword and miraculous loaf of bread.

"Can my son have been innocent?" the king thought to himself. "Alas, I am sick at heart." Out loud he said, "How I wish he were alive! I will never forgive myself for having him killed."

At that the huntsman spoke up. "He is still alive. I could not bring myself to kill him." And he told the king what had happened.

A weight fell from the king's heart. He immediately sent a proclamation throughout his kingdom saying that his son should come home, where he would be welcomed with happiness and love.

In the meantime, the beautiful princess had her servants build a road, made of pure and shining gold, that led straight to the castle gate.

She said to her guards, "The man who rides straight to me up the center of the golden road is the right man, and you are to allow him to enter. But any man who rides to one side or the other of the golden road is not the right man, and you are not to let him in."

When the year was almost over, the oldest son decided it was time to go to the princess. He expected to pass himself off as her savior, and so claim her and her kingdom for his own.

When he saw the golden road gleaming in the sun, he said, "It would be a terrible shame to ride on a road as wonderful as this." He turned his horse to the side, and rode up to the castle along the right side of the golden path.

When he reached the castle, the guards said, "You are not the right man." And he was turned away at the gate.

Closer to the year's end, the second son went off to claim the princess and her kingdom. When he came to the golden road and his horse had set just one hoof upon it, he said, "It would be a thousand pities for a horse to tread on a road as beautiful as this." And he rode his horse along the left side of the road.

When he reached the castle, the guards said to him, "You are not the right man." And he too was turned away.

At exactly the year's end, the youngest son decided to leave the forest and his sorrows behind him and go to his princess. He rode along thinking only of her, wishing only to be with her. And so when he came to the road he did not notice it was made of gold. He rode quickly right up the center of its shining surface, straight to the princess's castle.

When the guards saw this, they said to him, "You are the right man." They opened the gates wide to allow him to enter.

The princess greeted him joyfully. "You are my savior, and the lord of my kingdom."

They were married with great celebration and much rejoicing throughout the land.

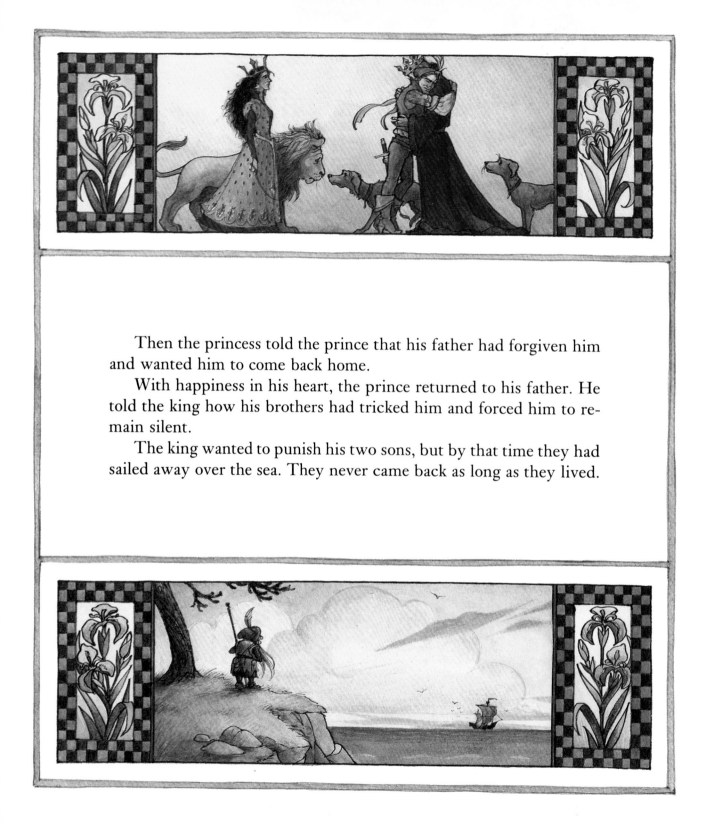

Then the princess told the prince that his father had forgiven him and wanted him to come back home.

With happiness in his heart, the prince returned to his father. He told the king how his brothers had tricked him and forced him to remain silent.

The king wanted to punish his two sons, but by that time they had sailed away over the sea. They never came back as long as they lived.